Twins Go to Bed

By Ellen Weiss
Illustrated by Sam Williams

ALADDIN
New York London Toronto Sydney

First Aladdin edition June 2004

ALADDIN PAPERBACKS
An imprint of Simon & Schuster Children's Publishing Division
1230 Avenue of the Americas
New York, NY 10020

Book design by Debra Sfetsios
The text of this book was set in Century Oldstyle.

Printed in the United States of America
2 4 6 8 10 9 7 5 3 1

Library of Congress Cataloging-in-Publication Data

Weiss, Ellen, 1949–
Twins go to bed / by Ellen Weiss ; illustrated by Sam Williams.— 1st
Aladdin pbk. ed.
p. cm. — (Ready-to-read)
Summary: Rhyming text follows a set of sleepy twins as they get into
their pj's, brush their teeth, and are tucked into bed.
ISBN 0-689-86517-1 (pbk.) — ISBN 0-689-86518-X (lib edition)
[1. Bedtime—Fiction. 2. Twins—Fiction. 3. Stories in rhyme.] I.
Williams, Sam, 1955– ill. II. Title. III. Series.

PZ8.3.W4245Ts 2004
[E]—dc21
2003011628

Day is done.

We had fun.

Made some noise.

Played with toys.

Now we are cranky.

We need our blankie!

Time for a book.

We can both look.

Just one more!

Or maybe four?

Pj's on.

Sun is gone.

Brush, brush, brush.

Do not rush.

Snuggle in bed,

sleepyheads.

Turn out the light.

Good night!
Good night!